P9-ELR-401

GOLDILOCKS, GO HOME!

GOLDILOCKS, GO HOME!

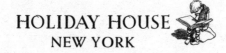

Martha Freeman

illustrated by
Marta Sevilla

HOLIDAY HOUSE
NEW YORK

Text copyright © 2019 by Martha Freeman

Illustrations copyright © 2019 by Marta Sevilla

All Rights Reserved

HOLIDAY HOUSE is registered in the U.S. Patent and Trademark Office.

Printed and bound in March 2019 at Maple Press, York, PA, USA.

www.holidayhouse.com

First Edition

1 3 5 7 9 10 8 6 4 2

Library of Congress Cataloging-in-Publication Data

Names: Freeman, Martha, author. | Sevilla, Marta (Illustrator), illustrator.

Title: Goldilocks, go home / by Martha Freeman ; illustrations by Marta Sevilla.

Description: First edition. | New York : Holiday House, [2019] | Summary:
Baby Bear and Goldilocks contentiously relate the events of an action-packed
week in the Enchanted Forest when Goldilocks stays with the
three bears waiting for the Big Bad Wolf to leave.

Identifiers: LCCN 2018016637 | ISBN 9780823438570 (hardcover)

Subjects: | CYAC: Characters in literature—Fiction. | Bears—Fiction
Wolves—Fiction. | Humorous stories.

Classification: LCC PZ7.F87496 Go 2019 | DDC [Fic]—dc23 LC record
available at https://lccn.loc.gov/2018016637

ISBN: 978-0-8234-3857-0 (hardcover)

To librarians who read aloud classics
old and new at story hour

CONTENTS

PROLOGUE

The Furless, Yellow-Haired Creature

Once upon a time there were three bears, Mama Bear, Papa Bear, and Bobby Bear, and they lived in a tidy cottage. Life was happy for the three bears.

I should know.

I'm Bobby.

That's not his real name.

Do me a favor? Pay no attention to the furless, yellow-haired creature.

His real name's Baby. He just thinks Bobby sounds more mature.

As I was saying. Life was happy for the three bears . . . until the day a furless creature with yellow hair who thinks she's so funny invaded their space.

After that, nothing was the same.

ONE

Why Did the Wolf Cross the Road?

My story begins on an ordinary Tuesday, the thirty-third morning in a row that Mama had made porridge for breakfast. (Before that, she'd been on a bark-and-beetles kick.) Papa and I looked at the porridge, and then at each other.

If you're wondering, porridge is a lot like glue. Only less tasty.

Hey, are you dissing my mama's cooking?

You want to know what I really hate?

Interruptions!

Now, where was I? Oh yes. Papa asked, "Who wants to go for a walk?" And then he whispered in my ear, "Maybe we can pick some blueberries—jazz it up a little."

I grabbed a basket, and out the door we went.

It was a lovely morning, and we saw lots of neighbors. The tortoise sat under a tree playing her harp.

The Pig Brothers went by, pushing wheelbarrows

loaded with bricks, sticks, and straw. Since they got their own show on HoGTV, those guys are always remodeling.

Farther along, the swan formerly known as ugly duckling admired his reflection in the pond.

When we got to the meadow, Coyote appeared ahead of us on the path. As usual, he had a joke: "Why did the wolf cross the road?"

I thought for a second. "Maybe he was chasing the chicken?"

Coyote looked disappointed. "You already heard this one."

"I hope it wasn't the little red hen," Mama said. "She's a hard worker, a real credit to the barnyard."

"Did the wolf catch the chicken?" I asked Coyote.

"You guys are a terrible audience. You know that, right?" Coyote said.

"We just want the chicken to be okay," I said.

"You'll have to ask the wolf about that," Coyote said.

"Oh, no," Mama said firmly. "Baby . . . that is Bobby will not be asking the wolf any such thing. Bobby is a good and careful little bear. He does not talk to strangers."

Coyote sighed. "I was trying to be funny."

"There is nothing funny about the wolf," Mama said.

"Time to move along?" Papa said.

"See ya, Bobby Baby," said Coyote.

"See ya 'round, clown," I said.

The best blueberries are by the bramble patch.
Cock Robin and his friends had picked them over, but

there were enough to improve porridge. My basket was almost full by the time we headed home.

So far, the morning had seemed like any other.

Little did we know the wolf was not the only threat that lurked in our woods. Little did we know there was an intruder.

TWO

Disaster Area

By now you've probably guessed the intruder's identity. She was none other than the furless yellow-hair we are currently trying to ignore. Her name? Goldilocks.

Hey there! How ya doin'? Party at the bears' house! Boo-ya!

Most of the time, creatures such as she do not dare enter our woods. This is for one good reason: the wolf.

TBH, we humans aren't that crazy about bears either. Bears are big, with claws and teeth. Besides that, they smell!

If we smell, how come you moved in with us?

Because wolves smell worse! Hahaha!

You see what I've had to put up with? It's more than a baby, I mean a *Bobby*, should have to bear—get it?

But let's get back to my story.

Not suspecting anything was wrong, Mama, Papa, and I returned to the tidy cottage. Only it wasn't tidy at all. It was a disaster area!

So I ate some porridge and broke a chair—get over it!

And where was the cause of the disaster?

We looked in the kitchen. We looked in the parlor. We looked in my bedroom—and there she was!

"Mama! Papa!" I cried. "Somebody's sleeping in my bed!"

I was startled, I don't mind saying. I had never before seen anything so furless. Was it a new kind of reptile?

Papa explained. "That, son, is a human. Female, by the looks of her."

Papa's deep voice must have woken her up. She opened her eyes. She sat up straight.

"Tell that human she's outta here!" I cried.

Mama looked at me sternly. "Bobby Bear, where are your manners?"

"You're right." I apologized. "Tell that human she's outta here *please*!"

THREE

Now a Word from the Virtuous, Fair-Haired Princess

Blah, blah, blah. Boring, boring, boring. Move over, Bobby Bear. It's my turn!

Once upon a time there was a virtuous, fair-haired *princess*—

> Ha! If she's a princess, then I'm Santa Claus.

—named Goldilocks who, owing to some cosmic mistake, was being raised by humble peasant folk in a gated community in the burbs.

Even though Goldilocks did not live like a princess, she was happy.

She liked Grimm Elementary School where her teacher was a witch, but not a wicked one.

She liked her best friend, Jack, who was good with plants, particularly beanstalks.

She liked her kung fu lessons with Mulan, and her cooking classes with the butcher and the baker.

Every Saturday, she went to the library for story hour with Scheherazade. Her favorite books were realistic fiction.

Fairy tales, you mean.

The story of the virtuous, fair-haired princess begins once upon a Monday after school. She and the peasant woman were having a quarrel. Never mind the reason for the quarrel.

Aren't you dying to know what the reason was? I figured the yellow-hair did something horrible. I figured her mother threw her out!

Are you even listening? I did not say mother. I said peasant woman. And the argument—whatever its cause—was a doozy. Yelling, crying—the works!

At last the fair-haired princess had had enough. "No one around here even loves me!" she declared. "I am running away to find my real parents, the king and queen, and my real house, the castle."

"Do give it a rest, Goldi, honey," said the peasant woman. "Who besides family would put up with your drama?"

The peasant woman tried to catch the princess in a hug, but the princess slipped from her grip and stomped right out the door.

"Be home for dinner," the peasant woman called. "We're having wild-boar burgers, your favorite. Oh— and whatever you do, stay out of the woods!"

The peasant woman's words gave the princess an idea. She wasn't sure where to find the castle, but the woods were a good place to start.

FOUR

Worst of All: The Wolf!

Over the years, the virtuous, fair-haired princess had heard many stories about the woods.

Is it just me? Or does all
this "virtuous princess"
stuff make you want to
toss your porridge?

Her friend Vasilisa said a witch
named Baba Yaga lived there in
a house built out of bones. The

twins, Hansel and Gretel, said yes, there was a witch, but her house was made of gingerbread, and you'd better not sneak a bite.

Momotaro, a new boy at school, said never mind witches, there were demons in the woods, and one day he and his friend the talking dog would take them on.

The walk to the woods took the princess beyond the mall to the burbs' far reaches. Along the highway she passed Aladdin's Lighting Store, Cinderella's Shoes, and Ali Baba Flooring.

Just past the Sleeping Beauty Thousand-Winks Motel she stopped at a footbridge spanning a brook. On the other side were trees and shadows—in other words, the woods.

The princess thought of the stories she'd heard: the witches; the demons; and worst of all, the wolf!

He was clever. He was hungry. He had sharp claws and vicious teeth.

The princess's heart went thud.

A wild-boar burger sounded pretty good.

Should she turn back?

Yes.

No! Not all of us are good and careful all the time, Bobby. Some of us have guts.

You mean like greasy grimy gopher guts?

Not that kind of guts. The kind that gives you courage!

Squaring her shoulders, the princess took one step, then another onto the bridge. She was halfway across when a deep and gravelly voice called out from below: "Halt! Who goes there?"

FIVE

Who Goes There?

Great job, furless one. Very suspenseful. So let's get back to the story everyone's been waiting for—my story. The next morning—

Hang on, Bobby! I'm not done yet!

Are you serious?
Two whole chapters
you've used up.

Never mind him. Where was I? Oh yes, as I was saying: "Halt! Who goes there?"

The princess stopped in her tracks. "I think I know this one," she said. "Can you give me a hint?"

"No hints."

"In that case, I give up. Who goes there?"

"I am the one who asks questions," said the voice. "You do not ask questions."

"Why not?" the princess asked.

"Because . . ." the voice began, then stopped. "Hey wait, that was another question!"

"Hahaha—I wondered if you'd notice." The princess took three steps and then the bridge began to rumble.

"Who goes there?" demanded the voice.

By this time the princess was annoyed. "Sheesh— I hope not everyone in the woods is as big a grumpy pants as you."

"I am not a grumpy pants!" said the voice. "I am a troll!"

And you know what? He really was! The princess found this out a moment later when he appeared before her, blocking her path.

SIX

A Manicure Would Do Wonders

Now, I don't mean to be mean, but this troll was really unattractive—pale green skin and a bad buzz cut straight out of the fifties.

Nice talk from a princess.

I'll thank you to keep your opinions to yourself, Bobby Bear.
You wouldn't know a princess if one bit you.

Oh, so now you're a vampire?

If I was, I wouldn't bite *you*. *Bleahh!* Bear fur. Yuck.

As I was saying, the virtuous fair-haired princess as usual remembered her manners and extended her delicate hand.

"It's very nice to meet you, Mr. Troll," she said. "I believe we have a mutual friend. Do you know the Beast? He hangs out with one of my BFFs, Beauty. No one's clear exactly what their status is, if you get my drift, but rumor has it—"

"**Silence!**" the troll cried.

For a moment after that, the only sounds were birds singing and leaves rustling. Soon, though, the princess's kind heart got the best of her.

"You know something? A manicure would do wonders for those gnarly fingers, and I bet you could use a pedicure, too, only please please please don't show me your toes. Anyway, you want my advice, you'll go see Thumbelina. She works at Rapunzel's Let-Down-Your-Hair Salon."

The troll studied his fingernails. "I am overdue," he admitted. "But who shall I say sent me?"

"Oh no." The princess shook her head. "I'm not falling for that one'"

The troll was big and scary. But the princess was quick. Without further ado, she made like an NFL prospect: faked right, spun left, and ran for daylight up the middle.

"See ya later, Mr. Troll—not!" she called back. Then almost before she knew it, she was smack dab in the woods.

SEVEN

I Hope the Castle Has Twinkle Lights

Night fell, and it was very, very dark, because—guess what—there are no streetlights in the woods.

Also no streets.

Feeling her way, the princess wandered up one path and down another. Soon she was cold and hungry, tired and lonely.

Finally, virtuous (and fair-haired) though she was, the princess had to admit she was lost.

"I hope the castle has twinkle lights," she said to herself. "If it doesn't, I'll walk right by and never see it."

No sooner had she uttered these words than she saw a light in the distance. What a cool coincidence if it turned out to be the castle!

You mean a cool coincidence like the ones that happen in fairy tales?

Not all fairy tales. Because this light was small and low to the ground, nothing to do with a castle at all. Indeed, as Goldilocks watched, she saw that it was bouncing along.

I know what it was! I know! I know!

Fine. Impress us with your knowledge.

It was Kitsune, the fox, playing with his ball of fire.

He's right! Score one for the furry short guy!

Sadly, the friendly light soon faded, and the rising moon spread spooky, ghastly shadows. Soon the princess began to shiver.

And that's when something horrible happened.

EIGHT

Fuzzed!

Did you meet the wolf?

No, not the wolf.

Then it can't have been
horrible. Woods-wise,
the wolf is the only
horrible thing.

Ha! Says you! What happened was horrible too! I will bet you a bowl of blueberries.

A sticky, creepy, fly-specked, scary, clinging, disgusting **spider web**! Which grabbed on to the princess's face in the dark, and would not let go!

I know, right?

After the princess got done screaming, she looked around for the spider and got mad. "I will squash you like the bug you are!"

"But I am not a bug," the spider replied. "I am an **arachnid.**"

"Squash you like an arachnid, then! I never saw your web at all—then wham-o I got fuzzed!"

Shuddering, the princess tried to wipe away the schmutz.

"That's what you get for having only two eyes," the spider said. "Anyway, my apologies. My web is meant to trap insects not children."

"I'll have you know I am a princess."

"That's what they all say. How did you get past the troll? Didn't he ask, 'Who goes there?'"

"I wouldn't tell him," the princess said.

"Very tricky," said the spider. "And I should know. Anansi's my name, and tricks are my game. If you had told him, he would've been allowed to eat you."

"Who made *that* rule?" said the princess.

"Other trolls, I guess. So what brings you to the woods?"

"I'm looking for my real parents. They live in a castle. Do you know them?"

"Are they humans like you? Known to carry scepters and wear crowns?"

"That's them!" said the princess, overjoyed. Maybe finding her real parents would be easier than she thought.

"Never heard of 'em," the spider said. "Anyway, humans don't live in the woods. Everyone knows that."

The princess choked back a sob. "I didn't know that, and if it's true, it means I'll never find my real parents. Plus I'm cold and I'm tired. And it's dark. And I haven't had my supper—"

"Enough, already!" For a spider, Anansi was not very patient. "You whine more than some doomed flies of my acquaintance. Tell you what. Take the next left, and you'll come to a tidy cottage. Maybe someone there will take you in."

Poor princess. Little did she know the spider was playing a trick.

The tidy cottage wasn't to the left at all; it was straight ahead.

Finally, after wandering all night, she came to it in the morning. By then she was too tired even to wonder who lived there. When no one answered her knock, she tried the door and found it was unlocked.

NINE

A Trio of Large and Fearsome Animals

Can I just ask one question? Why do you call yourself "the princess," anyway? Why not just say "I" like normal people—or normal bears?

Because "the princess" is more poetical.

If you say so. But you're not really—

Don't say it, Bobby.

I mean, no diss, but the truth is you're not—

I *said* don't say it! This is *my* part of the story, and in *my* part of the story, I can be whoever I want.

Now, where was I? Oh yes, once she was inside, the virtuous fair-haired princess—

Aw, sheesh.

—encountered porridge, chairs, and beds. Some of the porridge, frankly, was not up to princess standards, but one bowl—

Mine.

—was just right. So she ate it.

Similarly, two of the chairs lacked something in the comfort department. But one chair—

Mine.

—was just right. Sad to say, it suffered from poor workmanship and soon fell apart the tiniest bit.

Broke in a thousand pieces, she means.

By this time the princess was sleepy and sought a bed. Once again, she found three. Two were inadequate. But the third—

Guess whose?

—was darn comfy. In no time the virtuous princess fell into dreamy slumber—

Snoring like a diesel.

—only to be awakened by a trio of large and fearsome animals—one mama, one papa, and one baby.

Grrrr.

Being as brave as she was virtuous, the princess was not one bit scared. Still, she was relieved when the mama spoke up. "Nothing to worry about, dear. Except for the occasional insect, we are vegetarian."

And that is the end of Part One. Thank you, thank you, thank you very much. I'll be here all week.

That's what I'm afraid of.

TEN

Go Ahead, Scare Her

Sheesh, did you think she'd ever be quiet?
Now, where did I leave off?
Oh yes. Chapter Three.

Are you serious? You can't go back to Chapter Three. You have to pick up the story here at Chapter Ten.

How come?

Because if you don't, the millions of kids reading this book will get confused and then annoyed, and then they'll tear the pages into pieces and crumple them and throw them away—and that would be wasteful.

For once, I guess the furless one is right. We will begin at Chapter Ten. As you'll remember, the yellow-hair is lounging around in my bed, and Mama Bear is being unnecessarily kind: "Poor little human. Alone all night in the woods. Tell me, dear, did you meet the wolf?"

"Hush now. Don't scare her," Papa said.

"Go ahead. Scare her," I said.

"I met the troll and a tricky spider named Anansi. Does the wolf have a name?" the human asked, rubbing her eyes."

"Big Bad Wolf, duh!" I said.

"Unfortunate name," said the furless one. "I bet he gets teased all the time at school."

"A wolf in school?" I laughed. "That's ridiculous!"

"Funny comment from a bear wearing cargo shorts," she said.

"Oh yeah? And what's your name?" I asked.

"Goldilocks."

"And you're making fun of Big Bad?"

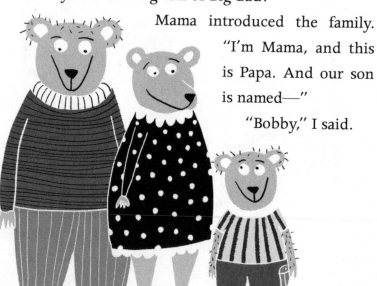

Mama introduced the family. "I'm Mama, and this is Papa. And our son is named—"

"Bobby," I said.

Mama sighed and looked at me. "If you say so."

"Nice to meet you," said Goldilocks, then she pushed back the covers and stretched. "Thanks awfully for the porridge. Have your people send mine a bill for any damage. And now, can you tell me— how do I get to the castle? I'm a princess, and my real parents live there."

I'd never heard of any castle, but I wanted the fur-less one gone. I was the baby—er, that is the Bobby— around here. This cottage was not big enough for both of us.

I pointed at random. "The castle is that way!"

"Are you sure you want to go to the castle?" Mama asked.

"Aha!" Goldilocks said. "So it *does* exist! The spider tried to trick me about that, too."

"Maybe not trick you. Maybe protect you," Papa said.

"I recommend you return to the burbs," Mama said. "Only there is one big, bad problem."

ELEVEN

Stay Away from the Castle!

At that moment I was feeling pretty confused.

Story of your life, right?

Oh, come on. You were confused, too. Was there a castle or wasn't there? Was it possible humans lived in the woods?

Precisely the questions I was about to ask Mama and Papa, but then—

Mama took Papa by the paw. "Excuse us a minute," she said. "We will be right back."

Now that we were alone, Goldilocks looked at me curiously. "I never met talking bears before," she said.

"I never met silent bears," I said. "And I thought all humans wore red coats with hoods."

Totally different story.

Well, I *know* that now. Then I poked you with my claw just to see if maybe you actually were a reptile.

And I squealed.

My ears are still ringing.

And Papa called from the hallway, "What's going on in there?"

And we both answered at the same time: "Nothing!"

"Nothing!"

A moment later, Mama and Papa came back with the announcement that ruined my life.

Not!

"Miss Locks," said Mama. "We have bad news. There's a wolf that roams the woods between our cottage and the bridge. This wolf leaves grown bears alone, but smaller creatures he sees as . . . how to put this delicately—tasty snacks. We'd like you to be our guest till the new moon, the first moonless night. You'll be safe if you leave then."

Goldilocks still didn't get it. "What about the castle?" she asked.

"Stay away from the castle!" said Mama and Papa. Then they growled to show they were serious.

"Oh!" said Goldilocks.

"Oh!" said I.

By now Goldilocks was on her feet. "Thanks awfully, but I can't possibly stay. The humble peasants would worry, and besides, I didn't bring a toothbrush."

Papa Bear shook his head. "I'm afraid we must insist. Big Bad Wolf only roams by moonlight. When it's dark he stays in and orders Chinese takeout. If you leave before the first moonless night, something bad might happen, and we would feel just awful."

"Not that awful," I said.

Goldilocks gulped. "In that case, it looks like you've got yourself a houseguest."

"Where's she gonna sleep?" I wanted to know. "What's she gonna wear? She's not sharing my toothbrush."

"Bobby Bear." My mama spoke sharply. "Didn't we raise you to be generous?"

"Generous to *bears*," I said. "This is an outrage!"

"You'll get over it," Papa said. "Now, who else is ready for breakfast?"

You will recall that someone had devoured mine. Mama offered to fix a fresh bowl, but I didn't really want it. What I wanted was to stomp around and kick things and glare.

That was a bad, bad morning. And there was worse to come.

TWELVE

Guess Who Had to Sleep on the Floor?

It turned out the new moon was a whole week away—the longest week of my life.

It was no picnic for me either, you know.

At night, Goldilocks wore my spare pajamas.

When it rained, she borrowed my raincoat.

And talk about a klutz! That broken chair was just the beginning. She was like a tornado with hair.

The worst part was my parents: Maybe Goldilocks wants more porridge. Maybe Goldilocks would prefer a different bedtime story. Would Goldilocks like an extra blanket?

Bobby might as well have left the island.

And guess who had to sleep on the floor? Hint: She never woke up with splinters in *her* tail.

To top it off, the human had a bad case of insomnia. Tossing and turning, turning and tossing—it was like sharing a room with a salad.

It's not easy being green.

Remember that first night? How you woke me up?

I had questions!

Yeah, like: Are you awake, Bobby?

And I wasn't. I mean, ever heard of a little thing called hibernation?

"What do you want?" I said. "It better be an emergency."

"It's the wolf," said the human.

I was up like a shot. "The wolf—where?"

"*About* the wolf, I mean. I want to know if he's really bad."

"Did you seriously wake me for that? Of course, the wolf is really bad."

"But what if the wolf thinks *we're* bad?" Goldilocks asked.

I rolled over. "Then the wolf is wrong."

"Maybe the wolf is just misguided," she said.

"Have it your way," I said. "But *bear* in mind—get it?—the wolf *does* want to eat us."

"Where's the evidence?" Goldilocks said. "Do you know anyone that's ever been eaten by a wolf?"

"How would that work? I mean, if they were eaten, I couldn't know them. At least not anymore."

"Answer the question."

"No. Okay? No," I said. "I do not know anyone that's been eaten by a wolf."

"I'm not sure I even think the wolf is real," said Goldilocks. "I think he's a story parents made up to keep cubs and children out of the woods."

THIRTEEN

Does the Wolf Talk, Too?

Is it my turn yet?

Your turn for what?

To tell the story my way.

Stop! Stop! Stop! Hold on, Furless, and let me have a turn.

The virtuous, fair-haired princess—

No-o-o-o!

—had a few more questions: "Since bears talk, does the wolf talk, too?"

"Of course not," said Bobby. "The wolf is an animal."

"But *you* talk," said the princess.

"Do I have to spell it out for you?" said Bobby. "I am a bear—b-e-a-r. A wolf is a wolf—w-o-l-f. Totally different letters."

Unconvinced, the princess pressed on. She wanted to know how come Papa, Mama, and Bobby wore clothes.

"To cover our bear bodies," he said.

"And where do you get your clothes?"

"At the store. Aren't there stores where you live in the burbs?"

"Of course. Malls, too," said the princess. "Where are your stores? I want to see. Can we go shopping sometime?"

"How 'bout if I ask *you* something for a change," the

bear said. "What would happen if I went with you to the stores in the burbs?"

"Uh . . . I guess you could," the princess said. "But I'd have to put you on a leash. Otherwise people might be scared."

"And how would you like to go to the store on a leash?" he asked.

The princess was wide-eyed. "I wouldn't!"

Bobby Bear shrugged. "There's your answer."

"What about school?" she asked. "You wear clothes, so do you go to school?"

"What's school?" the bear asked.

The princess guessed she had asked a dumb question. "So I guess you don't know how to read?"

"What's read?" Bobby asked.

Now the princess felt bad. Bobby Bear was just a dumb animal, after all. She hoped he wasn't insulted.

But before she could either apologize or explain, he laughed. "Hahaha—gotcha! Of course, I know how to read. What do you think I am—bar*bear*ic?"

FOURTEEN

Baby's My Job Description

After a few days in the tidy cottage, the princess began to feel at home.

"I like it here," she told Mama Bear. "Everything is just right."

I see what you did there.

Unfortunately, Bobby still wasn't used to having a houseguest. Basically, he was a selfish little bear—

—and did not play well with others—

—until the virtuous, fair-haired princess came into his life. She was, if I do say so myself, a very good influence.

One morning after breakfast, Bobby and the princess were having one of their occasional mild disagreements—

A big fight,
she means.

—and Bobby said, "We all know how the story goes. You're supposed to leave."

"Don't worry," said the princess. "Only a few more days till the new moon, and then I'll be out of your hair, uh . . . that is, fur."

Things got worse before lunch. Mama Bear was making Bobby's bed. Papa Bear had gone out gathering. Bobby and the princess were playing Go Fish on the floor—and using real fish.

How else would you play?

"Let me get this straight," said the princess between turns. "Your mama cooks and cleans. Your papa keeps the bees and gathers. What I don't get is your job, Bobby. What do you do around here?"

"I'm the baby," he said. "It's a tough job, but someone's gotta do it."

"But now you call yourself Bobby," said the princess.

"*Bobby's* my name. *Baby's* my job description. So, at your house, what's your job?"

"Custodial engineer," said the princess. "I empty wastebaskets, set the table, sweep my room, fold the laundry—"

Bobby held up a paw to stop her.

"When do you have time to be the baby?" he asked.

"I'm not a baby, Bobby. Would it kill you to make your own bed?"

Plumping Bobby's pillow, Mama Bear looked over. "This is the way we bears have always done things."

"What if there's a better way?" the princess asked.

Mama said, "Hmmm," as she tucked in a corner. "I'm going to think about that."

FIFTEEN

Unbearable

My turn!

Is, too!

Is not.

Is not.

Look. Can we make a deal? I take some chapters, then you, then me, then you—

Right. It works when we play Go Fish. Otherwise all this arguing will be boring for the millions of kids reading this book. I mean, it would be more efficient if we—

You do?

Wait—you, Goldilocks, are saying that I, Bobby Bear, actually have a good idea?

So where were we? Oh, yeah. The next morning. That's when furless wonder almost went too far. That's when she dissed the porridge.

You already know the porridge had issues. But Papa and I would never have complained. Complaining is not the way bears roll.

The human at the table was different. "Blueberries or no blueberries, porridge gets a little boring after a while," she said. "Don't you guys have sugar?"

"We have honey," Mama said.

"Of course!" said Goldilocks. "Could we have honey on our porridge?"

Mama raised her fur-brows. No bear had ever thought of such a thing. "I suppose we could try," she said.

"Not bad," said Papa after a bite.

"Pretty good," said Mama.

"Meh," I said. It tasted delicious, but no way would I admit that. You may have noticed Goldilocks is a know-it-all. Say something nice, and she gets un*bear*able.

Not funny.

When breakfast was done, Papa suggested that he and I take a walk.

"Am I going to get a lecture?" I asked.

"We are going to have a chat," he said.

"Why doesn't Goldilocks get a chat?" I asked.

"Goldilocks is our guest," he said.

"If I hear that one more time—" I said.

"Look, Bobby," said Papa Bear, "I know you're used to being top bear, but think how Goldilocks feels. She's far from her home, and her mama and papa."

"Let her take her chances with the wolf then," I said. "Have you seen the damage since yesterday? At this rate, you'll spend my college fund replacing broken dishware."

Papa ignored this. "It's good that everyone's different," he said. "Goldilocks has verve, while you are a good and careful little bear."

I could not believe what I was hearing from my very own father. "Just call me a wimp, why don't you? If you like her so much, maybe she should stay, and I should go live in the burbs. At her house, I might be appreciated."

"Your mama and I appreciate you," Papa said. "And we also appreciate Goldilocks."

"That's it," I announced. "Wolf or not—I'm going."

And away I went—straight up the path and into the shadows.

SIXTEEN

You're Making This Up!

He didn't get very far.

Hey! It's still my turn!

So sorry. Continue.

Now, where was I?

On the path.

Right!

But I didn't get very far.

I was wondering about my new life in the burbs. Was the furless one's house full of broken furniture? How was the porridge?

Then, from deep in the woods, I heard a sad, sad sob. It was enough to break your heart. So, I left the path to investigate. Brambles caught my fur, and briars scratched my skin. Pebbles and acorns bruised my paws.

You gotta wonder which one of us is really the princess, right?

At last I came to a clearing, and there he was.

The king of beasts himself!
The lion!

Get out! You're
making this up!

I'm not!

He was curled up like a kitten,
head resting miserably on the ground,
tears dampening his whiskers.

"What's the matter,
your majesty?" I
asked. "May I be
of assistance?"

"No one can help me," he whimpered and showed me his paw. Embedded in it was a thorn.

"Owie," I said.

"Guess I'll just lie here and die," said the lion.

The woods are full of princesses these days.

"Hang on a sec," I said. "I know just the guy we need."

Off I went and soon returned. "King of Beasts, meet Mouse. Mouse, meet the king of beasts."

The lion's reply was a pitiful moan. "No animal so lowly can help a majestic creature such as myself."

"Three words, your majesty: tiny rodent incisors."

The mouse moved fast. I mean, wouldn't you? And before the lion could argue further, the operation was complete, the thorn removed.

"Feeling better?" I asked.

The lion inspected his paw. "Much better—and hungry, too. Mice are talented surgeons *and* delicious appetizers. Now where did your little friend get to?"

"Wait, what?" I scooped up Mouse to protect him. "You can't eat him, your majesty. He did you a big favor!"

The lion chuckled. "A little royal humor is all. I am grateful for your assistance, Mouse, and for yours as well, Bobby Bear. Mark my words: I won't forget this."

Is there supposed to be a moral to that story?

Stay tuned. Meanwhile, helping the king had pretty much used up my energy for running away to the burbs. Not to mention, I hadn't packed a lunch. I returned to the path, and guess who was standing there?

Papa Bear?

No, not Papa Bear. It was you! Don't you remember?

Is that when we had the fight?

Bingo. You said I should be grateful for the whole honey-on-porridge thing. I said, What about cavities? What about empty calories? What about packing on pounds?

And I said, In your case, no one would notice a few pounds here or there.

And I said, Are you calling me overweight?

And I said, If the T-shirt fits or more like if it doesn't fit anymore—

And so on.

I felt pretty angry. I guess so did you.

Got that right. And I felt something more: determination. Same as the mouse removed the thorn, I vowed to remove *her*.

SEVENTEEN

What Even Is a Grub, Anyway?

Bobby Bear tried everything to get rid of the virtuous, fair-haired princess.

He put pepper on her porridge, but she called it a delightful twist on an old favorite.

It turns out humans have something called the "Food Network."

He dropped one of Anansi's eight-legged cousins in her underwear drawer.

The spider and Goldilocks told each other jokes.

He put a rubber snake in her bed.

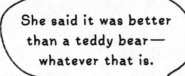

She said it was better than a teddy bear—whatever that is.

Meanwhile, Bobby's dad kept right on with the whole peace-love-and-harmony bit. "Here's an idea," he said at dinner. "Let's think about all the things that bears and humans have in common."

"Good thinking," said Mama. "I'll start. Humans and bears both eat blueberries and porridge."

"Indeed, we do," Papa said. "And don't we all enjoy a tasty grub now and then?"

The princess's stomach lurched. "*Ewww! No!* What even is a grub anyway?"

"Hahaha—what a kidder, Goldilocks," Papa said. "Everyone knows that grubs are like worms, only juicier and not so skinny."

"Mmmm," Mama said, rubbing her tummy. "I wish I had a dozen right now!"

The princess pushed away her plate.

"What's the problem?" Bobby wanted to know.

"The problem is that's disgusting!" she said.

Mama Bear tried to change the subject. "So, tell us something special that you like to eat."

"Lots of things," she said. "Like, uh . . . bacon. I really like bacon."

"Never heard of it," Bobby said.

The princess could not believe this. "You know—salty and crisp and comes in strips? Made from pig meat?"

Bobby and Papa shuddered. "*Ewww!*"

Mama said, "Perhaps you didn't know that the three pigs are our neighbors. Nice guys with their own houses and a show on HoGTV. Personally, I don't see why bachelors need all that square footage, but I guess a pig's home is his castle."

Did somebody say "castle"?

"Speaking of which," the princess said, "I don't suppose you've changed your mind about letting me go look for the one in the woods? I'm still hoping to find my real—"

"*No!*" Papa said.

"The subject is closed," Mama said.

Ha! That's what they thought. No one else knew it, but I was having a brainstorm.

EIGHTEEN

Bobby "Bad Boy" Bear

Are you wondering what my brainstorm was?

 No.

Fine. Be that way. I'm still going to tell you.

What a surprise!

My brainstorm was this: What if I gave Goldilocks what she wanted—took her to the castle? When we got there, her real parents, the king and queen, would claim her, and she'd be gone from my life forever.

And how did that work out for you?

Not exactly the way I expected.

As anyone who's read this far knows, I am a good and careful little bear.

In fact, up till that morning, I had never once lied to my mama and papa.

But after a few days of life with the furless one, I was a changed cub. Desperate. An outlaw. Bobby "Bad Boy" Bear.

Which is why the next morning (Porridge: Day 39), I wasted no time putting my plan into action.

"Good morning, Mama. Good morning, Papa," I said politely as usual. "After breakfast, Goldilocks and I are going out to, uh . . . fetch a pail of water."

Papa gave me a funny look. "You do know we have indoor plumbing, right?"

"Don't discourage him," said Mama. "Up till now, he's never offered to lift a paw around here. Bobby, are you feeling okay?"

"I feel fine!" I said. "It's only a pail of water. It's not like I volunteered to scrub the toilet."

"Good idea!" said Goldilocks. "How about adding 'toilet' to your chore list for when we come back?"

I started to say, "Add it to yours!"—but then I remembered.

Goldilocks would not be coming back.

Cue the scary music.

Cue the thunder, lightning, and rain.

Wait, what? It wasn't that way at all.

Poetic license, okay?

Bobby, it was a beautiful morning. Blue sky. Daffodils. Birdsong.

Only who could hear the birdsong?

Goldilocks never stopped talking: "That's just great you volunteered to help out. I guess I've been a good influence, right? Hey—where's the pail? Don't we need it to fetch water? I hope the wolf is sleeping in. Am I ever glad to get out of that cottage!"

The yakking kept on, but I wasn't listening. I was thinking. How far was the castle?

Goldilocks was dishing about a stuck-up friend of hers—Snow Something—when we reached a fork in the path.

"Which way?" Goldilocks asked.

This was a very good question.

NINETEEN

Knock Knock!

So what happened next was Bobby stood there blinking for like maybe an hour.

Ha! Thirty seconds tops.

And the princess should have been suspicious, right? The guy had lived his whole life in the woods. Now he couldn't even find the pond?

Finally, Bobby said, "We're going this way because, uh . . . I have a surprise for you."

"Awesome!" the princess said. "What is it? Ice cream? Chocolate? I could really use some chocolate. Oh boy, I hope it isn't grubs."

"Better than grubs," he said. "I am taking you to the castle."

Now it was the princess's turn to blink. "Oh, Bobby Bear!" she said and threw her arms around him. "Thank you, thank you, thank you. . . . "

I had never been hugged by anything so furless. It was not a nice sensation.

Oh, yeah? Well, I'm lucky I didn't get fleas!

I'll have you know I shampoo twice a week.

Clean fleas are still fleas, you know.

Anyway, like I said, we were walking on the path, and Bobby explained, "We'll take Coyote with us. He's a clown, but he knows the woods. Also, since the wolf is Coyote's cousin, Coyote's not on his menu."

Coyote lives in a snug den between the briar patch and the pond.

When Bobby and the princess got to his door, Bobby hollered, "Knock knock!" and soon Coyote appeared.

"You know that's my line, right?" Coyote said.

"Pardon me, Coyote, but we don't have time for jokes," Bobby said.

"Story of my life. Who's the blonde?"

Bobby introduced the princess and explained that they needed help. When he mentioned the castle, Coyote turned pale—or as pale as a guy with a fur face can turn.

"You don't want to go there," he said.

"We don't?" Bobby said.

"We do," the princess said.

"Why don't we?" Bobby asked.

The princess glared at him. "I guess your mama and papa were right all along," she said. "I guess you are a good and careful little bear."

"What's wrong with good and careful?" Coyote asked.

"He's a wimp," the princess said.

"Nice talk," Coyote said. "Didn't your parents teach you manners?"

"My real parents are the king and queen," the princess said. "We are going to the castle to meet them."

"I never heard of any king," Coyote said, "but I can see how the queen might have been the one to teach you manners."

"Meaning just what exactly?" the princess asked.

"You'll find out soon," Coyote said. "The castle's not far. I'll show you the way, but when we get to the moat, I'm out. If you choose to go on, don't say I didn't warn you."

"But you didn't warn us," Bobby said.

"Hahaha—pretty funny for a cub," Coyote said. "Keep in mind, it's me that makes the jokes around here."

TWENTY

Nice Knowing You

Don't tell Furless, but I started having second thoughts the moment we set out.

You know I'm right here, right?

At first Coyote told blonde jokes—

Not funny.

—and after that he got quiet.
Too quiet.

Hadn't Mama and Papa warned us to stay away from the castle? And why had they kept it a secret all this time?

Still, I couldn't let Goldilocks think I was a wimp. I had to be brave.

We followed Coyote up the hill and down the dale, and then the fog rolled in.

More scary music?

You bet!

I had never visited this part of the woods, and I don't mind telling you it was spooky and bone-chilling. I was beginning to wish I had my winter coat when Goldilocks stopped in her tracks.

"OMG! There really *is* a castle!" Above the fog loomed spiky black towers and turrets.

I was flabbergasted. "Wait a sec—up till now you didn't believe the castle was real?"

"I wasn't sure," she admitted. "I thought maybe I made the whole thing up because I was mad at my mom, uh . . . that is, the humble peasant woman."

"Mad why?" I asked. "What was that quarrel about anyway?"

Before Goldilocks could answer, Coyote spun to face us and yipped. "Moat's straight ahead. Nice knowing you. Good luck—you'll need it!"

"What's up with him?" Goldilocks asked when Coyote had fled.

"I guess we're gonna find out," I said. "Hey—did you just see a shadow?"

We looked up. Vultures were circling.

I gulped. "It could be worse. It could be flying monkeys."

You should never have said that, Bobby. Because only a few steps later—

Hey! My turn! A few steps later, bigger and bulgier shapes flew over.

And they were making monkey noises.

Goldilocks kept her eyes on the path. "I don't even want to know."

"In that case, I won't tell you. Come on, let's knock at the drawbridge. It can't be any scarier inside than it is out here."

TWENTY-ONE

Won't You Please Come In?

Hahaha! I can't believe you actually said that. Talk about being totally wrong.

I'm not arguing. Only—

Only *what*?

Only we wouldn't have been there at all if a certain furless wonder hadn't wanted to meet her real parents.

Yeah, well. There's that.

So take your turn already! People are dying to know what was in the castle.

Okay, okay. First things first. It wasn't *what,* it was *who.* And they heard her before they saw her.

"Welcome children!" said a voice at the same time the drawbridge groaned and dropped open. "Won't you please come in?"

Bobby and the princess crossed the bridge and found themselves in a wide stone hall lit only by stubby candles. I don't mind telling you the princess's heart was pounding, and she grabbed Bobby's paw.

"Uh—hello-o-o?" the princess called.

"Olly olly oxen free?" Bobby tried.

"Greetings, children," said the voice, which was deep and throaty.

His was deep and *gravelly*.

The voice had come out of nowhere, but then an orb appeared, bright and indistinct, at the far end of the hall. Think a cross between Glinda's transport contraption and the beamer machine on *Star Trek*.

"Technically, I'm a cub," Bobby replied. "Not that we absolutely need to be technical."

"So sorry," said the voice. "Greetings, child and cub. Welcome to my humble abode."

Scared as she was, the princess couldn't help it, she snorted. "Hahaha! Humble? This place is huge! You could have the U.S. Army for a slumber party, and there'd be room to spare."

"It is spacious," said the voice. "But it's a burden as well. You just can't get good help these days. Sometimes I'm so desperate I'm tempted to pick up a mop myself."

"You should totally have servants," Bobby said. "Weren't those flying monkeys outside? Give them a pay raise, and they'll help."

Naturally, the princess disagreed.

Naturally.

And she said so.

"It's only fair you should help clean if you live here. Many hands make light work—that's what the humble peasant woman says."

"Which humble peasant woman is that?" the voice asked.

"The one who was raising me instead of my real parents."

"And who are your real parents?" the voice asked.

The princess took a breath and squeezed Bobby's paw.

"That's what we're here to find out."

TWENTY-TWO

Come Closer, Child and Cub

Picture the three of us poised in suspense. On one side, the glowing orb. On the other, the furless yellow-hair and the adorable cub.

Adorable?

Then, as we watched, the orb transformed itself into a human silhouette that gradually took on depth and color.

Within moments, Goldilocks and I were facing a woman wearing a gleaming crown, a jewel-bedecked gown, and pointy high heels.

"Come closer, child and cub," said the woman.

"Yes, ma'am." I ambled toward her. "I mean, that is . . . your highness."

If you want to know the truth, I was hungry. How about second breakfast in the banquet hall? I didn't know what queens ate exactly, but it was probably better than porridge.

Besides, a snack break would put off me having to face Mama and Papa. They wouldn't be happy that I'd been gone so long or that I'd come back alone.

Thinking Goldilocks was right behind me, I approached the queen. But then I felt a sharp tug in the region of my stumpy tail.

"*Ow!*" I squealed and looked back to see the

yellow-hair wide-eyed and gripping a handful of my fur. "What gives?" I asked. "That's gotta be her—your real mother!" "

Goldilocks was pale and staring. "Sorry, your highness," she said. "Case of mistaken identity. My bad. Come on, Bobby—we gotta go!"

"Without a snack—are you kidding?"

No, I was not kidding. The truth is, I had a bad feeling that we might be the snack.

Before I could say more, Goldilocks was halfway back to the drawbridge. Being Goldilocks, she had knocked over two chairs, a coat rack, and a lamp on her way.

Is it my fault stark terror makes me clumsy?

Dodging wreckage, I followed. I thought we were safely outta there until—*bang!* the drawbridge slammed shut! We were trapped!

TWENTY-THREE

You're the One with Claws

Behind us, I heard cackling—

> Never a good sign.

—and I don't mind telling you, I was scared.

But then I had a good thought: Sure, I'm only a cub. But I'm also a wild animal. And a wild animal ought to be able to vanquish an elderly human!

Who you calling elderly?

Wait one sec. Where did she come from?

Haven't you ever heard of a cameo appearance?

Well, cameo disappear!

I got right up in the queen's face. "Open the draw-bridge," I said, "and let us out right now!"

And did she?

Not exactly.

Instead, she said, "Oh, please," and rolled her eyes. "You are looking at a charter member of Wicked Queens International."

"I knew it!" Goldilocks said. "You're not my real mother at all."

"And I was doing so well faking nicey-nice. What gave me away?" she asked.

"Yeah, what?" I asked Goldilocks. "She looks like any other queen to me—not that I exactly hang with royalty."

"Too much eye makeup—*duh*," said Goldilocks. "Haven't you ever seen a Disney movie? The good queens go light on the liner."

The furless one was right about the makeup. When

the pulsating blob turned female, she sprouted lashes an inch long and dual blue-shadow stripes.

I was feeling clueless when Goldilocks cried out: "Be careful, Bobby! There's something in her hand!"

A dagger? A wand? A fazer?

None of the above!

"It's the drawbridge clicker!" said Goldilocks. "Grab it, Bobby Bear!"

"*You* grab it," I said.

"You're the one with claws," said Goldilocks.

"Good point," I said.

I see what you did there.

And after that, I wasted no time and batted the clicker away from the queen, caught it, closed my eyes, and *squeezed*.

TWENTY-FOUR

I'm Here to Fetch the Heart of the Little Girl

Wickedness isn't very powerful if it doesn't help a queen in a fight with a baby bear.

Hey, Furless, watch yourself. I'm a wild animal—grrrr.

No diss, Bobby. Just an observation. Anyway, no one likes wickedness.

Would someone get her out of here?

The clicker worked. The drawbridge opened. Bobby and the princess took off. That is, Bobby and I took off. It seems I am not a princess, after all. I am just me—Goldilocks.

Any second, I expected to feel the queen's clutches. But her highness tripped on her pointy high heels, and that's how we got away.

From the other side of the moat, I looked back and saw the queen skulking in the shadows.

"Give over that clicker!" she cried.

"My bad," said Bobby and lobbed it across.

"Why'd you do that?" I asked.

"It wasn't mine," he said. "Besides, I don't have a drawbridge."

A single path led away from the castle, the same one we'd followed with Coyote. I was afraid the flying monkeys might strike, but they must have been out on banana break. Soon the fog was behind us, and we were in sunshine. I thought we were safe until something on a tree branch caught my eye—a gleaming white crescent, a smile without a face.

If you're thinking Cheshire Cat, you're thinking wrong.

It was the Cheshire *Crocodile*! And before we could go another step, it had shinnied tail-first down the tree and blocked our way.

"Look, crocodile," Bobby said. "We have just escaped from the wicked queen. Compared to her, you're small potatoes. Now move aside before I get annoyed."

The crocodile flashed his teeth and snapped his jaws.

"Maybe medium potatoes," Bobby said. "What is it you want, crocodile?"

"Funny coincidence, but that queen is my boss," he said, "and I'm here to fetch the heart of the little girl."

"You know that's gross, right?" Bobby said.

I was too scared to speak.

"Look, cub, I just work here," the crocodile explained. "Now hold still, young lady."

The crocodile slithered my way, and I thought I was a goner.

But then Bobby Bear spoke up. "Wait a sec—here's the thing. The furless one forgot to bring her heart with her."

"W-W-Wait, what?" I said.

"And what's more, she can prove it. Go ahead," Bobby commanded. "Show him you don't have a heart."

I figured for furless, that would be easy.

Have I mentioned you're not funny?

I stuck my hands in my pockets and turned them inside out.

"Nothing in here but lint," I said.

The crocodile sighed, and tears welled in his eyes. "I'm going to be in big trouble when I return to the castle empty-clawed again."

"What do you mean *again*?" Bobby asked.

"You'd be surprised how many creatures travel without their hearts," the crocodile said.

"Here's a suggestion," Bobby said. "Maybe you could deliver *your* heart instead, crocodile. Would the queen know the difference?"

The crocodile admitted that this was indeed a suggestion. A bad one, but a suggestion.

"Or how about this?" he asked. "What if I quit my job with the queen and come with you? I'm not the smartest reptile in the swamp, but I have strong jaws and a good work ethic."

"It's okay with me," I said. Pretty much any solution that did not require giving up a body part was okay with me.

"You could ferry us across the lake on your back," Bobby said. "It's easier than going around."

What can I say? Letting the crocodile come with us seemed like a good idea at the time.

I thought so, too. I mean, what could possibly go wrong?

TWENTY-FIVE

Can't Catch Me!

Bobby here, with a partial list of things that go wrong when you travel with a crocodile:

1. He threatened to eat Brer Rabbit.
2. He threatened to eat Tanuki, the raccoon.
3. He threatened to eat the goose that lays the golden eggs.

We had to take turns talking him out of things. Brer Rabbit is too stringy, I explained. Tanuki is too tough.

Those golden eggs are murder on the tummy.

"I wish we'd meet up with the big bad wolf," Goldilocks said. "If the crocodile ate him, I could go home to my real parents in the burbs."

"Don't you mean the humble peasant persons?"

Goldilocks sighed. "I guess they were my real parents all along."

"*Now* you tell me," I said.

"Maybe we needed to go on a quest to achieve personal growth," Goldilocks said. "Don't you think you're a little less wimpy? And I'm a lot more careful."

"Careful?" I said. "What about the heap of broken furniture at the castle?"

Right then a flat brown cookie with piped icing and currant eyes shot out of the shrubbery.

"Can't catch me! I'm the gingerbread man!"

"Yummy!" said the crocodile. "Can I at least eat *him*?"

"Not if I can help it!" called Kitsune the fox, who was hot on the big cookie's trail.

"Go for it and good luck," I told the crocodile. "For a baked good, that guy is really annoying."

Goldilocks and I watched the crocodile take off in a hurry.

"There goes our ride across the lake," she said.

On the long walk home we were quiet.

Honestly? I was feeling pretty bad. I mean, wouldn't you if you'd just found out you weren't really a princess?

I don't want to be a princess.

But think of all those tiaras!

Meanwhile, I used the walk to think up an excuse for why we were so late. Soon I had invented a gripping tale about the frog prince, the Loch Ness monster, and a giant peach. Sadly, I never got to tell it. Approaching the tidy cottage, Goldilocks and I saw Mama and Papa out front, wringing their paws.

"We were worried sick!" Mama cried before squishing us in a big bear hug.

"It looks like the western woods aren't enough for the wolf anymore," said Papa. "He's been prowling our neighborhood, too."

"Those poor Pig Brothers have lost two houses," said Mama. "But where have you been all this time? Honestly, I don't know whether to give you porridge or put you in time-out."

TWENTY-SIX

We Didn't Get Eaten

The porridge tasted so good—

We were really hungry.

—that I told them the real story.

"When Goldilocks and I returned to the tidy cottage," I concluded, "Mama and Papa Bear fed us lovely porridge, and generously forgave us for everything. The End."

That last part was poetic license.

Yeah, it was. Because Mama and papa were scowling.

"You disobeyed us!" said Papa Bear.

"*And* you fibbed!" said Mama Bear.

"But we didn't get eaten," I reminded them.

When Mama and Papa continued to scowl, I began to feel bad.

"I won't lie anymore," I said. "It's wrong, not to mention super stressful."

"Promise?" Mama said.

"Cross your heart?" Papa said.

I did.

So did I.

And everything would've been great—except *you* had to keep on with the promises.

"Bobby will also make his own bed every morning—"

"I will?"

"And dust the parlor on Tuesdays, and scrub the toilet—"

"Wait just one minute. What are *you* going to do, Furless?"

"I'd love to help out," she said, "but, alas, I won't have time. The new moon's two days away, and soon I'll be going home."

Don't tell, but the idea of Goldilocks leaving made me just a little bit sad.

Aw, gee, Bobby.
That's really—

I mean, who was gonna help me dust and scrub?

TWENTY-SEVEN

Wolf Soup

TBH, I was so glad to be back in the tidy cottage, I forgot all about the wolf's attack on the Bacon Boys.

Who?

The Pig Brothers, I mean.

Luckily, Bobby remembered. "What's the story with the wolf and the pigs?" he asked. "Are the three of them okay?"

Papa Bear did not draw out the suspense. The big bad wolf had trashed the houses of two Pig Brothers, and the guys had barely escaped with tails and trotters.

This all sounded familiar.

"Was one house made of straw and the other of sticks?" I asked. "Was huffing and puffing involved?"

Papa's Bear's round eyes got rounder. "How did you know?"

"Story hour at the library," I said. "And there's no time to waste. If all three are in the brick house now, we'd better get over there fast."

The big brick house was only a hop, skip, and jump from the tidy cottage.

Not surprisingly, the porkers looked peaked when they answered the door.

"Good to see you," the first pig said. "After what's happened, we're kind of freaking out."

Mama nodded kindly. "The wolf freaks us out, too, and we have sharp teeth and claws."

"Besides that, bears are not made out of tasty bacon," I added.

Talk about awkward. You should've seen the looks the pig gave her.

Tell me about it. I felt really bad.

Mama Bear took over. "Little pigs, meet Goldilocks," she said. "Goldilocks, meet the pigs."

"Can I just say I love your show?" I said. "Talk about barnyard chic! I am probably your *biggest* fan! But if you hope to be renewed for next season—or even survive till dinnertime —we have work to do. The wolf is going to come back. When he does, he'll try to blow this house down. Only it won't work."

"Of course it won't," the first pig said. "My brick house was built to last."

"Oh, get over yourself," said the second pig. "Who

knew the wolf would go all weather system? That's not usually how he operates."

"Usually, he grabs you by the throat and chomps," the third pig explained.

"Thank you for sharing," I said. "Either way, he'll be back. And when huffing and puffing fails, he'll try to get in through the chimney."

The pigs stared for a moment then started to laugh.

"You've mixed up your stories," the first pig finally said. "It's Santa Claus with the chimney. You know— red suit? Reindeer? Normal-size teeth?"

"We don't have time to argue," I said. "Put a kettle on the fire to boil, and when the wolf comes down the chimney—*splash!*—you've got wolf soup."

And then what happened?

No, he sure didn't. Instead, he said, "Little pigs, little pigs! Let me come in!"

TWENTY-EIGHT

I Guess We're on Our Own

The pigs didn't know the next line, so Goldilocks coached them. "No, not by the hair of my chinny chin chin," she whispered.

"No, not by the hair of her chinny chin chin!" they chorused.

That's what happens when you don't have time to rehearse.

The wolf, at least, picked up his cue: "Then I'll huff! And I'll puff! And I'll blo-o-o-ow your house in!"

All of us were trembling with fear.

All of us except Furless.

Working fast, we put the kettle on the fire and filled it with water.

Meanwhile, the wolf blew up a windstorm. The rafters and windows shook, but the house did not fall down.

Score one for brick and mortar.

At last the wolf ran out of hot air and the wind died. It was quiet. We looked at one other. Were we safe?

Had you even been listening to me?

We were not safe. There was a *thud* from above and the echo of *scritch-scratching* claws from the fireplace. The wolf was on the roof!

It was then that I made a miscalculation. I thought of how the wolf must feel. By the chimney in the cold, he was peering into the soot, thinking of bacon dinner, never suspecting he had in store a hot and watery death.

I mean, he was big and bad and a wolf—but no one deserves to boil!

What could I do? I had to stop him.

"Wait, Mr. Wolf!" I hollered. "Don't come down—it's a trap!"

The *scritch-scratch* stopped, four paws *pit-patted*, and the wolf leapt to the ground.

"It was the human's idea, I bet!" he called. "Look out, yellow-hair! I'll be back!"

Meanwhile, Mama, Papa, and the Pig Brothers were glaring at you-know-who.

I mumbled, "So sorry," and looked at Goldilocks. "Didn't you say the wolf's misguided? He might not be evil at all."

"I said that before he threatened *me*," Goldilocks said.

"What does story hour say we do next?" the first pig asked.

"It doesn't," Goldilocks said. "According to story hour, the wolf's dead and you're living happily ever after. From here on out, I guess we're on our own."

TWENTY-NINE

A Note on My Pillow

Was it a mistake for me to save the big bad wolf?

Yes.

Because of me, he would be back.

Because of me, Goldilocks was in danger.

Like I said.

At dinner that night, I tried to explain. "It's not as if wolf soup would taste good. What about the fur? What about the teeth? What about the horrible screams of pain?"

Does the word "wimpy" ring a bell?

No one answered, and I felt terrible.

After dinner, Mama did the dishes while Papa watched the Cubs on TV. Fur and teeth brushed, I went to my room expecting another night on the leaky old air mattress while Goldilocks did her tossed-salad routine in my bed.

Only Goldilocks wasn't there.

Instead, I found a note on my pillow.

Dear Bobby Bear,

I am leaving.

I mean, actually, since you're reading this, I have already left.

Tell your mama and papa thank you.

They were very kind to take in a yellow-haired, furless stranger.

Thank you for sharing your room and for going with me to the castle.

Actually, thank you for everything except saving the big bad wolf.

Since it wouldn't be fair to stick around and endanger you, Mama, Papa, and the tidy cottage, I am leaving before the new moon.

It has been nice knowing you. It has been nice being your friend. If you're ever in the burbs, look me up—on the off chance I survive, I mean.

Cordially,

Your furless, yellow-haired wonderful friend—Goldilocks

P.S.—Don't bother coming after me. Face it, you don't have the courage.

I put the note back on my pillow.

I felt sad.

I felt lonely.

I felt annoyed!

But I felt something else, too.

A surge of courage.

It was enough to push me down the hall, through the kitchen, and out the door.

After that, my natural wimpiness returned.

In the dark woods, bats swooped, owls hooted, and the moon played shadows with the trees. When Kitsune the fox yipped for her husband, I jumped.

I thought of the cottage, safe and warm. I thought of my very own bed.

Then I thought of Goldilocks. She was yellow-haired and furless and thought she was so funny. But she needed my help. And she was going to get it.

THIRTY

No Time for Discussion

I bet you're thinking Goldilocks never would have left the tidy cottage unless she had a foolproof plan.

I wasn't thinking that.

But the truth is I didn't have one . . . unless you consider Run Real Fast to be foolproof.

Which it wasn't.

I never counted on the consequences of so much porridge. Not to mention days without P.E. class. I was out of shape.

Also, she's a klutz, remember.

Soon I was breathing hard and stumbling over roots and rocks in the dark. When I stopped to catch my breath, I heard running steps behind me. I thought that I was done for!

"Don't hurt me, Big Bad Wolf!" I cried. When I turned to look, there was Bobby Bear. "Oh," I said. "Only you."

"Sorry to be a disappointment," he said.

"Story of your life, right?"

"You're so funny I—"

"—forgot to laugh. I know, Bobby. I know all your shtick."

"Is this the appreciation I get? Never mind rescue. I am going home."

"No, wait," I said, and reached for Bobby's paw. "The truth is I'm scared."

I couldn't believe you'd admit that.

Weren't you scared, too?

Terrified. But we've already established that I'm a wimp.

And I'm a klutz. No wonder we're such a great team.

"Together we escaped the wicked queen," Bobby reminded me. "We can escape the wolf, too. Come on!"

Unfortunately, the wolf disagreed and told us so just then with a hungry, blood-curdling howl: *Aw-rooooh!*

It was coming from far away, but still my heart went *thud*.

"T-T-Tell me again how we're going to escape?" I said.

"No time for discussion—*run!*"

Bobby was fast on two legs, but I teetered, wasting precious time.

Furless was also easy to track. That human scent is like a neon sign: Good Eats!

If I was ever going to see the burbs again, I needed a better plan, and soon I thought I had one.

"Wait, Bobby. Let's stop here and cry '*Wolf!*' Someone's bound to come and help us."

"Didn't they cover that at story hour?" Bobby asked.

"Or how about this?" I said. "We find a woodsman, and chop-chop-chop?"

Bobby made a face. "That's as bad as boiling. Also sexist. Why not find a woodswoman?"

Bobby reached back and tugged me along, but by now it was too late. Another howl told us the wolf was closing in, and then his stinky stench filled the air. I looked back over my shoulder and—yikes— was I sorry. Crashing through the brush came Big Bad himself. His black pelt gleamed. His red eyes glowed. Slobber dripped from his long white teeth.

And that's when something unbelievable happened.
Bobby abandoned me!

Before I knew what was happening, he'd dug his
claws into a tree trunk and shinnied into the branches.

Suddenly, I was by myself on the path, facing the
wolf alone.

THIRTY-ONE

Wolf Kibble

Oh, come on. You didn't think I'd for real leave
Furless by herself, did you?

I mean, annoying
as she was, I didn't
want her to end up
wolf kibble.

Thanks.
I think.

Agile as a circus bear, I flipped upside down, spread
my claws, caught her by the collar, and yanked.

It wasn't easy. The girl is heavier than she looks. If I'd fallen, the wolf would've chomped both our necks— and boy, would I have been in trouble with Mama and Papa!

As it was, Big Bad circled the tree trunk, snarling and snapping, then finally sat down and shook himself. "No problem," he said. "I will be right here. Eventually you'll fall asleep and lose your balance and fall. When you do—" He smacked his lips.

"Shouldn't you be grateful?" I asked. "If it weren't for me, you'd be leftover soup by now."

"Sure, I'm grateful," the wolf said. "Come down and I'll give you a hug. Bring the blonde snackable with you."

He was lying, Bobby Bear.
He wasn't grateful at all.

Yeah, I know that, thanks.

Just checking. Sometimes you are kind of gullible— and I mean that in the nicest possible way.

Now I worried the wolf might be right. What if we fell asleep? Besides that, we'd soon be hungry and thirsty. Was the tree that saved us really a trap?

Hey, whose turn is it?

As I was saying, No.

No, it was not a trap.

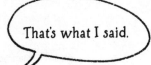

That's what I said.

I know, but you were stepping on my line!

Well, that's better than what you're doing.

What am I doing that's so terrible?

Slowing down the pace! Here. Let me help. What happened next was—

Oh, no you don't. It's my turn. What happened next was this: From down the path came a very large, very loud *roar*.

And it was a wonderful sound.

THIRTY-TWO

Three Bites

It was like we'd called 9-1-1 or something. He just figured out we were there.

They don't know who you're talking about.

They do if they're paying attention. I mean, earth to readers, who is it that roars, anyway? Hint: Last seen in the company of a mouse.

It was the lion, the king of beasts—

—who soon came sauntering along all awesome and majestic in the moonlight.

I decided to keep it casual. "Your majesty," I said. "Great to see you. How's the paw?"

"Much better, thank you," the lion replied. "And how are you, Bobby Bear?"

"I'm good," I said. "I mean, the big bad wolf chased my friend and me up this tree and now we're trapped, and he's planning to eat us. Otherwise, not a lot going on."

"Glad to hear it," said the king of beasts. "So I guess there's nothing I can do for you? I owe you a favor, remember."

"Oh, right, that thing with the festering wound and ginormous thorn," I said. "No, we're good. That is, unless you'd like to scare the wolf away? Or reduce him to a quivering mass of teeth and fur? My yellow-haired friend was hoping to go home to the burbs, and I wouldn't mind returning to my loving mama and papa. But if your plate's full, NP. We'll catch you later."

The king of beasts had been too busy looking up at me to notice the wolf on the ground. Now he did, and I kind of hoped he'd snarl and say *scram*.

Instead, he yawned.

Not a good sign. I mean, better than cackling. But still.

The wolf, that kiss-up, spoke fast: "Your majesty. How handsome you look!"

The lion didn't answer except to yawn again.

"Sleepy, your majesty? I mean, you're nocturnal, but even kings are entitled to catnaps. Can I get you a pillow?"

"I'm not yawning," the lion said. "I'm measuring. By my calculations, a wolf your size is about three bites—three and a half tops."

The wolf began to tremble. "You mean you're going to eat me?"

"Swallow you whole is more like it. No offense, but you're not good enough to chew."

"Uh, do I have a say in the matter?" the wolf said. "Just asking."

"Probably no . . . unless—"

"Unless what?"

"Unless you want to leave here so fast it's not worth my breath to chase you."

The lion did not have to say more. Already, the wolf was gone.

The furless one had been quiet all this time. Now with the danger past, she hollered after the wolf, "Don't even *think* about following me to the burbs! If you did, you'd have to cross the bridge first, and—wait a sec." She looked at me.

"Uh-oh." I knew what she was thinking.

We had both forgotten the troll.

THIRTY-THREE

Run for It, Furless!

Bobby and I climbed down from the tree and thanked the king of beasts.

"Uh . . . just one thing, your majesty, while I've got you," said Bobby. "How do you feel about the troll that lives under the bridge?"

"That guy? He's beastly, but not one of mine. Besides, Bobby, I only owed you one favor. You wouldn't want to push it with the king." The lion yawned again.

"Absolutely not," Bobby agreed. "Great hanging with you, your majesty. Have a pleasant evening!"

The lion went one way, we went the other. Soon we arrived at the bridge.

The voice from beneath was as deep and gravelly as ever: "Who goes there?"

Before I could shush him, Bobby answered. "My name is Bobby Bear!"

"No!" I squealed. "If you tell him your name, he can eat you! That's the rule."

"Will you pipe down a sec? I've got this," he said.

The deep and gravelly voice spoke again: "That name doesn't ring a bell. Is it the one on your birth certificate?"

"Look, troll, I ought to know my own name," Bobby said.

"Because if it's not, and I eat you"—the voice sounded thoughtful—"I'm pretty sure I lose my job as keeper of the bridge."

"Okay, okay. I admit it. My real name is . . . wait for it . . . *Rumpelstiltskin!*"

The troll seemed to ponder that. Meanwhile, Bobby whispered in my ear. "You're not the only one who goes to story hour. Now run for it, Furless!"

Already it was too late.

Rumbling and grumbling, the troll appeared on the bridge.

"Now I *know* you're pulling my leg," the troll declared.

"And such a handsome leg, too," Bobby said, "if gnarly and hairy is your thing, that is."

Meanwhile Bobby had been shoving me forward, yelling, "Get moving!"

"But we haven't said goodbye!"

"And we never will if the troll finds out my real name. Now *go!* Go! Go!"

I'm a klutz, remember. But I also watch ESPN. Calling on hours of study, I faked right, spun left, and ran for daylight.

You blew past that troll so fast I almost felt sorry for him.

I know, right? He was as confused as a rookie from a no-name school.

"Goodbye, Baby Bear!" I called from the far side.

At the same time, the troll slapped gnarly palm to gnarly forehead. *"Baby Bear! That's* your name!"

"Yep—gotta go," Bobby said.

And I never stopped running till I reached the tidy cottage.

THIRTY-FOUR

If It Looks Like an Invader and Cries Like an Invader

Didn't Mother Goose say, "Parting is such sweet sorrow, emphasis on the sweet."

Hahaha, Bobby Bear! Act all tough if you want, but anyone can see you missed me.

On the contrary, Furless, I never missed you one bit. That morning when I thought you were gone for good was the happiest of my life. Then the troll lost his job on the bridge—fired for twice letting you get away— and now you come visit when the moon is new and Big Bad's safely in his den.

But I still have a couple of questions. How about the humble peasant folk? Did they miss you?

Of course they did! Mom went to the police the same night I left. Sgt. Bo Peep predicted I'd come home wagging my tail behind me, and she was right—except for the tail part. What's your other question?

That fight with your mom—the reason you left in the first place. What was that about?

Do you promise not to tell?

It'll be our little secret— you, me, and the millions of kids reading this book.

It turns out that soon I'm going to be a big sister. I was pretty upset when Mom told me.

You mean your mom's expecting a cub?

In the burbs, we call them babies, Bobby. Oh, but you knew that already. After all your real name—

Don't say it!

What? Is the troll still around?

No way. I hear he got a gig with some billy goats. The point is now you'll have to do what I did—get used to an invader in your own tidy cottage!

It won't be so bad.

That's what *you* think. Getting along with an alien invader? Sharing your stuff? Sharing your room? Sharing your mama and papa?

Mom says the new baby will be sweet. Mom says it won't be an invader at all.

Get real, Goldilocks. If it looks like an invader and cries like an invader. . . . Anyway, I can't wait till you're not number one anymore. But after a while, you'll get used to it. I did. I even learned to like you in the end.

Speaking of which, this is the end of my story.

Your story?

Okay, fine, *our* story—the furless one's and mine.

But there is just one more thing. If I was the kind of bear who liked to show off with big words, I would call it an epilogue.

EPILOGUE

Another Furless Female

One Sunday after Goldilocks left, the Bears were on TV. Papa and I were dozing in front of the game when Mama came in from the kitchen. She had a broom in one paw and a dustpan in the other.

"Lunchtime so soon?" Papa asked.

Imagine our surprise when Mama growled!

"Wh-Wh-Wh-What?" Papa said.

Mama handed him the broom. "The kitchen floor needs sweeping, and Bobby's bed is still unmade. As for me, I'm going to put my paws up."

I was straightening sheets when I heard a knock at the door.

"I'll get it!" I volunteered.

Mama called from the parlor. "Probably one of the Pig Brothers. I offered them my recipe for porridge."

Papa was sweeping the front hall. "Unlikely to be a Pig Brother then," he muttered.

I opened the door, and there was another furless female. This one had a basket over her arm.

She squealed when she saw me. "A bear!"

"Where?" I said. "Haha—sorry. I crack myself up. Yes, I am a bear. And you appear to be a human. They're everywhere all of a sudden—like cockroaches, if you don't mind my saying so."

The furless one shook her head. "In fact, humans and cockroaches are very different. Humans are mammals. Cockroaches are more like termites."

"Did not know that. Thanks for stopping by." I started to close the door.

"No, wait!" she said. "My grandma lives in the woods, and she's sick. I'm supposed to deliver a get-well basket, but it's so heavy, and now I'm lost."

She looked ready to cry.

Mama Bear took over. "Come in, you poor thing. Here, let me hang up your hoodie. What do you call

163

that shade of red? It's really bright. Can I get you some porridge?"

The furless one took a seat at the kitchen table. At least she didn't break any chairs.

Papa sat down, too. "Let me get this straight," he said. "Your grandma lives in the woods?"

The furless one nodded.

"That can't be right," I said. "Only one human lives in the woods, and—" I had a terrible thought. "Wait a second. How much eye makeup does your grandma wear?"

THE END

COMING SOON . . .

LITTLE RED HOODIE

←———•———→

Martha Freeman

illustrated by
Marta Sevilla